Naval Warfare
of the
Revolutionary War

Diane Smolinski

Series Consultant:
Lieutenant Colonel G.A. LoFaro

Heinemann Library
Chicago, Illinois

Designed by Herman Adler Design
Printed in Hong Kong

06 05 04 03 02
10 9 8 7 6 5 4 3 2 1

Library of Congress Cataloging-in-Publication Data

Smolinski, Diane, 1950-
    Naval warfare of the Revolutionary War / Diane
Smolinski.
        p. cm. -- (Americans at war. The Revolutionary War)
    Includes bibliographical references and index.
    ISBN 1-58810-275-0 (lib. bdg.)
    ISBN 1-58810-561-X (pbk. bdg.)
    1. United States--History--Revolution, 1775-1783--
Naval operations--Juvenile literature. [1. United
States--History--Revolution, 1775-1783--Naval
operations. 2. United States--History, Naval--To 1900.]
I. Title. II. Series: Smolinski, Diane, 1950- .
Americans at war.
    Revolutionary War.
    E271.S675 2001
    973.3'5--dc21
                                        2001001619

Acknowledgments
The author and publishers are grateful to the
following for permission to reproduce copyright
material: p. 4, 28, 29 Corbis; p. 5, 12, 15 The Bailey
Collection: © The Mariners' Museum, Newport News,
VA; p. 6, 7, 9, 21, 22, 23, 26, 27 North Wind Picture
Archives; p. 8, 11 top, 19, 20, 25 top The Granger
Collection, New York; p. 11 bottom, 17 Collections
of The Navy Department Library; p. 16 Collection
of The New-York Historical Society, no.73212; p. 18,
25 bottom Culver Pictures

Cover photograph © North Wind Picture Archives

Every effort has been made to contact copyright
holders of any material reproduced in this book. Any
omissions will be rectified in subsequent printings if
notice is given to the publisher.

About the Author
Diane Smolinski is a teacher for the Seminole
County School District in Florida. She earned B.S.
of Education degrees from Duquesne University and
Slippery Rock University in Pennsylvania. For the past
fourteen years, Diane has taught the Revolutionary
War curriculum to fourth and fifth graders. Diane
has previously authored a series of Civil War books
for young readers. She lives with her husband, two
daughters, and their cat, Pepper.

Author's Note: Special thanks to my husband for the
idea to include a book on naval history in this series
and for his help with the research and writing.

About the Consultant
G.A. LoFaro is a lieutenant colonel in the U.S. Army
currently stationed at Fort McPherson, Georgia. After
graduating from West Point, he was commissioned in
the infantry. He has served in a variety of positions
in the 82nd Airborne Division, the Ranger Training
Brigade, and Second Infantry Division in Korea.
He has a Masters Degree in U.S. History from the
University of Michigan and is completing his Ph.D
in U.S. History at the State University of New York
at Stony Brook. He has also served six years on the
West Point faculty where he taught military history
to cadets.

Some words are shown in bold, **like this.**
You can find out what they mean by looking in the glossary.

Contents

Revolutionary War Naval Warfare

From 1775 to 1783, North American colonists fought the British for control of a land that was rich in raw materials and economic opportunities. This war for America's political independence was called the American Revolutionary War, or the American War of Independence. Events in this book were chosen to explain the importance that ships and their crews played in determining the final outcome of the war.

Importance of Waterways

There were few roads within the colonies during the 1770s, and they were usually in poor condition. The colonists depended on ships to carry goods for trading. At the beginning of the war, the British Navy controlled the coastline of the North American colonies.

Great Britain collected a tax on goods traded in the colonies. These taxes raised the cost of many items. To avoid paying taxes, some colonists tried to **smuggle** goods past British Navy ships.

British ships brought troops to Boston to restore order when colonists stopped paying their taxes.

Town Crier News

In the 1760s, the British government established several new taxes on colonists to help pay Britain's war debts.

- The Sugar Act of 1764 taxed molasses shipped to colonial ports.

- The Stamp Act of 1765 required merchants to pay to have important papers marked with a required stamp.

- The Townshend Acts of 1767 placed taxes on items brought into the colonies.

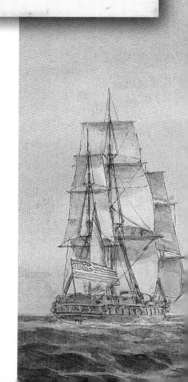

The Birth of the U.S. Navy

Early in 1775, some individual colonies decided to create navies to protect their **merchant ships** and ports from British warships. These navies consisted of small ships that sailed mainly within ports and inland rivers. They were not designed to fight the larger British Navy ships on the open seas. Some members of the **Continental Congress** wanted to **commission** warships that could defend seacoast towns and stop British raiding ships.

On October 13, 1775, the Continental Navy was created. The Continental Congress approved a plan to buy two merchant ships. Cannons were then mounted on the ships, turning them into warships. On October 30, 1775, Congress approved the purchase of two more ships. Esek Hopkins, an experienced merchant seaman, was appointed **commodore** of this small fleet.

The **frigates** *Raleigh and* Alfred *were some of the Continental Navy's largest ships. The* Raleigh *had 32 guns and the* Alfred *had 24.*

Shipbuilding in the Colonies

Even before the Revolutionary War began, shipbuilding was a major industry in the North American colonies. Since the soil along the seacoasts in the northern colonies was not good for farming, colonists turned to the sea to make a living.

The colonists became skilled at building ships. There were many large, tall pine trees in the nearby forests to use for making ship **masts.** Pitch, or sap from pine trees, was used as a waterproofing material to close up the **seams** between boards. Before the war began, the colonies had supplied the British with these same raw materials to build their ships. After the war broke out, it was difficult for the British Navy to get these materials.

Warships of the Continental Navy

Since the colonies did not have the money to purchase new warships, they relied on turning **merchant ships** into warships. To do so, they mounted guns on the ships. Merchant ships were often sturdy, but they were not as **maneuverable** as British warships.

Shipbuilding was an important industry in colonial North America.

Town Crier News

- It cost about half as much to build a ship in the colonies as it did to build one in Great Britain.

- One third of the ships used in British trade were built in the colonies.

- During the Revolutionary War, the number of cannons that ships carried usually determined the size of ships. Ships were armed with cannons that ranged in size from 3- to 36-pound (1.4- to 16.3-kilogram) guns. The term *pound* refers to the weight of the cannon ball.

Warships of the British Navy

The British Navy specifically built warships. These warships were faster and more maneuverable than **converted** merchant ships. Crews were better trained and in better health than those of the Continental Navy.

Meeting in Battle

One of the most common battle strategies at this time was for ships to sail next to each other and fire their cannons. Destroying the other ship's sails limited its movement. The attacking ship would then sail across the **bow** or **stern** of the disabled ship and fire again. The attacking crew could then board the disabled ship and capture the crew.

British warships sailed the waters near the North American colonies without any fear of the Continental Navy.

Privateers

During the Revolutionary War, the British Navy blockaded ports along the coast of the North American colonies. Privateers, which were fast, small ships, often slipped through the British blockade. They were able to bring war materials and supplies to the Continental Army. Privateers, also the name for the men who sailed on these ships, brought gunpowder from the West Indies and Europe to be used by George Washington's army.

Some of these ships were supported by the colonies. Most were owned by businessmen or wealthy merchants only interested in making money. Privateers attacked British **merchant ships** bringing supplies to the colonies. They then disappeared quickly into ports and rivers of the North American colonies. The larger British ships could not follow them.

Town Crier News

It is thought that more than 2,000 privateers attacked British merchant ships. They did about $18 million in damage to British businesses.

Privateers sold their captured cargoes to whomever would pay the most. Goods captured from a British merchant ship may have been sold back to British businessmen in the colonies. This caused prices to increase.

Better pay and fewer rules may have been some of the reasons that some colonial men chose to sail on privateer ships rather than join the Continental Navy.

Even though privateers disrupted trade of food and nonmilitary cargo, they were not able to stop most shipments of military supplies to the British Army. British military supply ships usually traveled with warships, which protected them from the privateers. Privateers caused many problems for British merchants and the British Navy, but they had little effect on the outcome of the war.

Ship captains of the Continental Navy had to compete with privateers to get crewmen for their warships. Privateers paid more and promised new **recruits** a share in the cargo they captured. This made it difficult for the navy to get the best sailors.

Town Crier News

The amount of pay received by Continental sailors during the Revolutionary War depended on the person's position.

Captain   32 colonial dollars each month

Gunner   15 colonial dollars each month

Seaman   6.67 colonial dollars each month

The Raid on Nassau

In February 1776, **Commodore** Esek Hopkins set sail with orders to drive the British from Chesapeake Bay. This was the first official voyage of the Continental Navy. Hopkins realized that his smaller ships had little hope of destroying the powerful British fleet. When it was reported that the British were storing gunpowder and arms in the Bahamas, Hopkins changed his course.

On March 1, 1776, Hopkins turned all eight ships of the new Continental Navy toward Abaco Island in the Bahamas. The Continental Navy hoped to capture gunpowder and arms for the **colonial** army.

Town Crier News

- Eight ships made up Esek Hopkins's fleet. They were the *Alfred, Columbus, Andrew Doria, Cabot, Providence, Hornet, Wasp,* and *Fly.*

- Esek Hopkins is considered the first **admiral** of the United States Navy.

Continental Navy ships, under the command of Commodore Hopkins, sailed 1,000 miles (1,609 kilometers) to the Bahamas.

First Attempt

Soon after the Continental Navy arrived in the Bahamas, they captured two ships owned by local British merchants. Hopkins placed armed sailors on both captured ships and sailed toward the forts that protected the Port of Nassau.

Unfortunately, Hopkins's fleet sailed too close to the port, and the men in the fort realized they were going to be attacked. They fired guns from the fort and drove off the Continental fleet. That night, the British loaded 150 barrels of gunpowder that had been stored on the island onto their ships. They sent it to safety in North America.

After a disagreement with the Continental Congress in 1777, Commodore Esek Hopkins (1718–1802) was dismissed of his command. In 1778, he was kicked out of the Continental Navy.

Second Attempt

Not realizing that the gunpowder was gone, **Commodore** Hopkins landed men on an **isolated** beach on the island. They marched across the island and attacked the forts from the rear. Both forts protecting the harbor were captured. Hopkins's men loaded 88 cannons, 15 **mortars,** 24 casks, or barrels, of gunpowder, 11,000 cannon balls, and 5,000 mortar shells onto waiting Continental ships. No men or ships were lost during this attack.

Before this attack, the British had been concerned that the French Navy was a threat to their resources in the West Indies. They now had reason to be concerned about the Continental Navy, too.

The Wasp *and* Frolic *were two ships used during the Revolutionary War.*

Town Crier News

Both marines and sailors landed on the beach at Nassau. This was the first landing of American troops on foreign soil from the sea.

1775	1776	1779
10/13 U.S. Navy created	**3/3 Raid on Nassau, Bahamas**	

Return to the Colonies

On March 16, 1776, Commodore Hopkins finished loading supplies captured at Nassau and set sail for the **colonies.** On the return voyage, about 200 sailors died from smallpox and fever. Due to poor diet and poor living conditions, disease was common on ships at this time. The loss of these sailors hurt the Continental Navy. There were not enough men available to sail all the ships.

On the return trip from the Bahamas, one of the original eight ships, the *Wasp,* had to stop in Philadelphia because it had been damaged in a storm. The rest of the fleet sailed for Newport, Rhode Island.

After Action Report	Continental Navy	British Navy
Military Leaders	Commodore Esek Hopkins	Governor Montfort Browne (political leader of Nassau at the time of the attack)
Ships Involved	8	2 captured **merchant ships**
*Casualties	200 (due to sickness)	3 prisoners taken back to the colonies
Outcome	victory	defeat

* Casualties include those who were wounded, killed, or missing in action. These figures are unavailable for some Revolutionary War battles, because the people involved did not always keep records of the numbers.

1780   1781   1783

Block Island, Rhode Island

After leaving the Bahamas on March 17, 1776, Hopkins's fleet arrived near Block Island Channel off the coast of Rhode Island on April 4, 1776. There, they met and captured two British warships, the *Hawk* and the *Bolton*.

Hopkins questioned the crew of the captured ships and found that the British fleet was sailing near Newport, Rhode Island. He was careful to avoid the main British fleet, but hoped that he might be able to capture other ships that had sailed away from the main fleet. Early on the morning of April 6, a lookout on the Continental Navy ship *Andrew Doria* spotted the sails of a British warship.

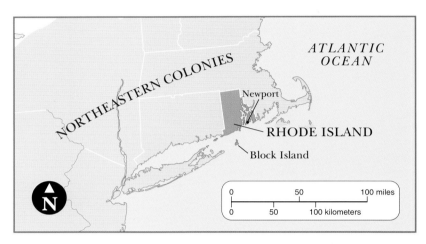

Block Island is located ten miles (sixteen kilometers) off the coast of Rhode Island.

April 6, 1776

The sails belonged to the British **frigate,** HMS *Glasgow*. The *Glasgow* sailed toward the Continental fleet to see if they were friendly or not. As the *Glasgow* approached, the **colonial** ships opened fire. The British warship was outnumbered seven to one. The *Glasgow* returned fire and tried to escape the Continental fleet. The battle and chase lasted several hours. The *Glasgow* damaged four Continental Navy ships. The *Glasgow* was also damaged and required major repairs.

Town Crier News

The Continental Navy had the advantage over the British Navy.

Alfred	30 guns	*Providence*	12 guns
Columbus	28 guns	*Hornet*	10 guns
Andrew Doria	14 guns	*Fly*	6 guns
Cabot	14 guns	*Glasgow*	20 guns
Total Continental guns: 86		**Total British guns: 48**	

Despite the odds being in their favor, **Commodore** Hopkins and Captain Hazard, of the *Providence*, were unable to defeat a single British warship. They were removed from their positions in the Continental Navy for their poor performance in this battle. The battle near Block Island was a serious setback for the Continental Navy. Captain Hazard's second in command was John Paul Jones. He became the captain of the *Providence* after Hazard was removed from the position.

After Action Report	Continental Navy	British Navy
Military Leaders	Commodore Esek Hopkins	Captain Tryingham Howe
Ships Involved	7—none destroyed	1—none destroyed
Casualties	10 killed, 14 wounded	1 killed, 3 wounded
Outcome	defeat	victory

The British frigate Glasgow *escaped from Commodore Hopkins's fleet at Block Island.*

1780   1781   1783

Battle of Lake Champlain

In late 1775, General Benedict Arnold led an army of **colonial** soldiers north into Canada. The colonial government hoped that Canada would become the fourteenth colony. Their goal was to drive the British from Canada, but Arnold encountered many problems. Food and ammunition quickly ran out, and many of his soldiers were wounded or lost in the wilderness. The invasion was unsuccessful.

Since there were few roads in this part of North America at this time, armies depended on rivers, lakes, or the ocean to move their troops quickly. In June 1776, Benedict Arnold put his men onto boats and retreated south across Lake Champlain. Upon reaching Fort Amherst, the soldiers were finally able to rest in safety.

Town Crier News

Before Benedict Arnold joined the Continental Army, he was a merchant. He sailed to the West Indies and Europe. He designed the ships used in the Battle of Lake Champlain based on ships he saw during his travels.

According to this 1776 map of the Colony of New York, few roads were built at this time. This is one of the reasons why it was important for the colonists to build a navy.

1775	1776	1779
10/13 U.S. Navy created	3/3 Raid on Nassau, Bahamas 4/6 Battle off Block Island, Rhode Island 10/11 Battle of Lake Champlain	

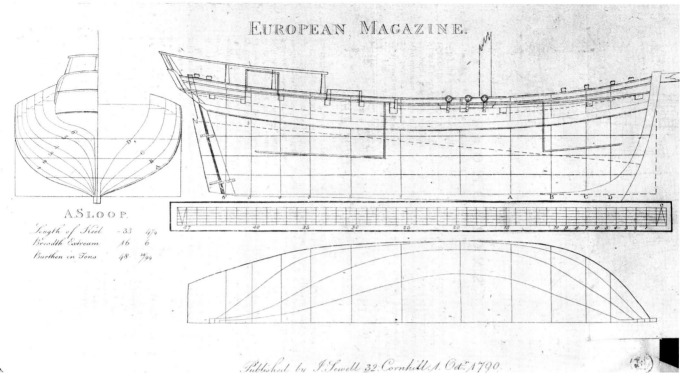

These design drawings show that a ship like the ones Benedict Arnold sailed could travel in shallow waters.

The British Plan

While fighting the British in Canada, Benedict Arnold discovered that the British planned to invade the Colony of New York and attack George Washington's army. The British planned to sail across Lake Champlain, Lake George, and down the Hudson River to New York in ships built to travel in shallow water.

Benedict Arnold convinced George Washington that the British had to be stopped on Lake Champlain. Arnold knew the British could not be defeated, but they could be slowed down. If the Continental Army could hold off the British Army until winter weather arrived, the British would have to give up the invasion until the following spring. This delay would give General Washington time to increase the size of his army or get help from France.

Town Crier News

The size of the British Army that planned to travel down Lake Champlain included 10,000 British **regulars,** 2,000 German **mercenaries,** 4,000 Iroquois Indians, and 1,000 Canadian men who had been conscripted, or forced to fight.

1780 **1781** **1783**

Building Ships

Benedict Arnold planned to build twenty small, fast ships. He would equip them with oars so they could move when there was no wind. Arnold's ships were built from materials close to Lake Champlain. Because of shortages of some materials and of skilled shipbuilders, only fifteen of these boats had been made by late September 1776.

Fighting Begins

On October 11, 1776, the British fleet sailed out onto Lake Champlain. Arnold hid his ships behind Valcour Island on the lake. At first, the Continental army used the advantage of surprise to damage some of the British ships. They attacked the British ships sailing past the island. But when the British turned their ships and fired their **broadside** cannons, they badly damaged the Continental fleet. The battle raged until nightfall.

Each of the boats involved in the Battle on Lake Champlain was designed a little differently from the others.

Town Crier News

The 15 Continental ships were no match for the 28 British ships on Lake Champlain.

1775

10/13 U.S. Navy created

1776

3/3 Raid on Nassau, Bahamas
4/6 Battle off Block Island, Rhode Island
10/11 Battle of Lake Champlain

1779

18

Invasion Delayed

As darkness fell, the British withdrew. They planned to finish the battle the next day. That night, Benedict Arnold and his damaged fleet slipped through the British line and headed south. They beached and burned the few ships that had survived the battle to keep the British from capturing and reusing them.

It took time for the British to repair the damage to their ships. When winter weather arrived, they decided to return to their winter quarters in Canada. Although Benedict Arnold had lost his fleet, he was successful in delaying the British invasion of New York until the following year. Most importantly, the delay gave General Washington time to gather and train troops.

Benedict Arnold was a hero at Lake Champlain and an important leader in the Continental Army for four years.

After Action Report	Continental Navy	British Navy
Military Leaders	Gen. Benedict Arnold	Gen. Sir Guy Carleton
Ships Involved	15—all destroyed	28
Casualties	60 (plus 320 captured)	40
Outcome	defeat	victory

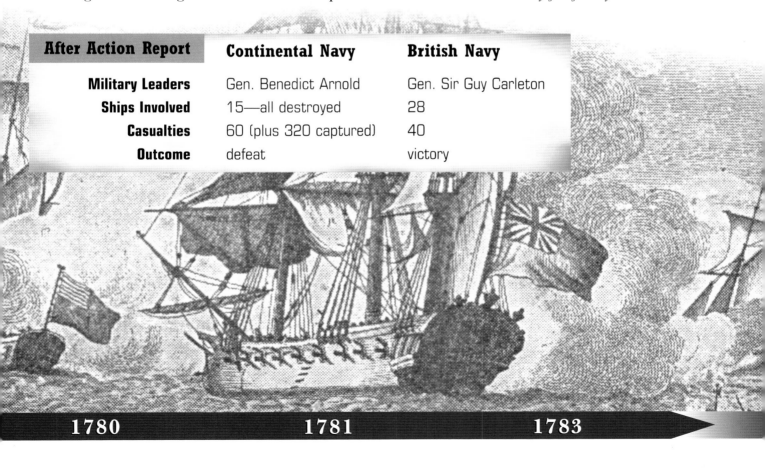

1780　　　　1781　　　　1783

Battle of Flamborough Head

Revolutionary War naval battles did not always take place along the North American coastline. The American ship commanded by Captain John Paul Jones, the *Bon Homme Richard,* and the British ship commanded by Captain Richard Pearson, the HMS *Serapis,* battled off the eastern coast of England, near Flamborough Head.

John Paul Jones commanded a small fleet of ships sent to attack **merchant ships** leaving England for the **colonies.** On September 23, 1779, Jones spotted a **convoy** of British merchant ships led by the *Serapis.* The *Bon Homme Richard* was an older, rebuilt ship with 42 cannons. It would have to match the new, 44-cannon British **frigate** *Serapis.*

The Battle Begins

The two ships moved into place to attack. Once in range, they both used their **broadside** cannons. At first, the *Bon Homme Richard* was badly damaged. Some of its cannons were destroyed, and some sails were shot off.

Town Crier News

• The letters *HMS* before the names of British ships stand for "Her (His) Majesty's Ship (Steamer)" or "Her (His) Majesty's Service."

• This is the only battle of the Revolutionary War in which the captain who won the battle lost his ship.

Captain John Paul Jones directs the crew of the Bon Homme Richard *during the battle with the* Serapis.

1775	1776	1779
10/13 U.S. Navy created	**3/3 Raid on Nassau, Bahamas** **4/6 Battle off Block Island, Rhode Island** **10/11 Battle of Lake Champlain**	**9/23 Battle of Flamborough Head**

The Bon Homme Richard *and the* Serapis *fire broadside cannons at the start of the battle.*

Despite the damage to his ship, John Paul Jones positioned it alongside the *Serapis,* and his men tied the ships together. Sharpshooters on the *Bon Homme Richard* fired muskets at the gun crews on the British ship. The *Serapis* continued to fire its cannons, even though the ships were tied together. Then, the *Bon Homme Richard* caught fire. Captain Pearson called for Jones to surrender. Jones answered, "I have not yet begun to fight." The battle continued for more than three hours. Captain Pearson surrendered. The crew of the sinking *Bon Homme Richard* boarded the *Serapis.*

After Action Report	Continental Navy	British Navy
Military Leaders	Captain John Paul Jones	Captain Richard Pearson
Ships Involved	7 (2 American, 5 French) The main ship, the *Bon Homme Richard,* sank.	2—none destroyed
Casualties	A total of about 200 men were killed or wounded.	
Outcome	victory	defeat (Pearson surrendered)

1780   **1781**   **1783**

The Fall of Charleston

Early in 1780, General Sir Henry Clinton sailed from New York City with nearly 8,000 British Army troops to attack Charleston, South Carolina. The Continental Army was in place to defend Charleston. The Continental Navy also sent the **frigates** *Boston, Providence, Queen of France,* and *Ranger* to help defend the city of Charleston against the British fleet. When the British fleet arrived, the Continental fleet was trapped in Charleston harbor.

The British Navy shelled the city with cannon fire from their ships while the British Army set up land **artillery** around the city. On May 12, 1780, after a month-long **siege,** the Continental Army surrendered Charleston.

The British first attacked Charleston in 1776, as illustrated here, but they failed to take the city at that time. They attacked again in 1780, and succeeded.

1775	1776	1779
10/13 U.S. Navy created	3/3 Raid on Nassau, Bahamas 4/6 Battle off Block Island, Rhode Island 10/11 Battle of Lake Champlain	9/23 Battle of Flamborough Head

The fall of Charleston nearly destroyed the Continental Navy and Army in the South. More than 5,000 soldiers and large amounts of equipment, supplies, and weapons were surrendered to the British. Also, the Continental Navy's last **squadron** of ships was still trapped in Charleston Harbor. These ships had to surrender to the British. The Continental Navy was no longer a fighting force that could attack British warships or keep the British Navy from moving troops and supplies easily.

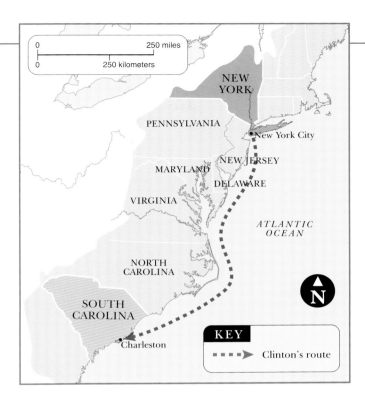

The defeat of the Continental forces at Charleston showed **colonial** leaders that they would need help to defeat the British. They decided to call upon the French, who had a large army and a powerful navy.

*The Treaty of **Alliance** was signed by Conrad-Alexandre Gerard of France and by three Americans—Benjamin Franklin, Silas Deane, and Arthur Lee.*

Town Crier News

- In a document called *The Treaty of Alliance*, France agreed to help the colonials fight the British in the American Revolutionary War.

- Charleston, South Carolina, was the most populated city in the southern colonies. About 8,000 people lived there at the time of the Revolutionary War.

| 1780 | 1781 | 1783 |

5/12 Fall of Charleston

The Siege of Yorktown

One of the naval battles that had a great effect on the outcome of the Revolutionary War did not involve any Continental Navy ships. It was, instead, the French Navy that drove the British fleet away from the Chesapeake Bay area.

In October 1781, General Cornwallis marched his British Army troops into Yorktown, Virginia. He was there to get supplies and fresh troops that General Clinton was supposed to send from New York City.

General George Washington hoped to trap Cornwallis at Yorktown and defeat him. Washington sent the French General Lafayette to block Cornwallis from leaving Yorktown by land. Meanwhile, the French fleet, under the command of **Admiral** de Grasse, arrived at Chesapeake Bay to prevent Cornwallis from escaping by boat on the York River.

KEY
→ British route
→ Colonial route
····· Colonial troops

NEW YORK
PENNSYLVANIA
New York City
NEW JERSEY
MARYLAND
ATLANTIC OCEAN
DELAWARE
VIRGINIA
Chesapeake Bay
York River
Petersburg
Yorktown

N

0   50   100 miles
0   50   100 kilometers

Cornwallis's troops were trapped in Yorktown. Their escape was blocked by land and by sea.

Town Crier News

- The French sent two fleets of ships for a total of 36 ships. The British had 19 ships.

- The surrender at Yorktown did not officially end the war. However, after the battle, the British were willing to negotiate peace.

1775	1776	1779
10/13 U.S. Navy created	**3/3** Raid on Nassau, Bahamas **4/6** Battle off Block Island, Rhode Island **10/11** Battle of Lake Champlain	**9/23** Battle of Flamborough Head

The British Surrender

After defeating the British fleet, French Admiral de Grasse positioned his fleet off the coast near Yorktown and began to bombard Cornwallis. General Cornwallis waited for help, but none came. He was surrounded, low on ammunition, and running out of food. On October 17, a British fleet left New York City with 7,000 troops to rescue Cornwallis. On the way, they met part of the French fleet and turned back to New York City. On October 19, 1781, General Cornwallis surrendered at Yorktown.

French Admiral Compte Francois Joseph Paul de Grasse (1722–1788)

The battle of Yorktown was the battle that brought an end to the Revolutionary War. General Washington's defeat of General Cornwallis was made possible with the help of the French Navy.

On September 5, 1781, the French fleet, led by Admiral de Grasse defeated the British fleet of Admiral Graves off the Virginia Capes.

1780	1781	1783
5/12 Fall of Charleston	10/19 Surrender at Yorktown	9/3 Treaty of Paris

Captain John Paul Jones (1747–1792)

John Paul Jones is considered the founding father of the U.S. Navy. He was one of the most famous people to serve in the Continental Navy during the Revolutionary War.

Early Years

John Paul Jones was born in Scotland in 1747. His name at birth was John Paul. He started work as a crewman on a British **merchant ship** when he was twelve years old. In 1769, John Paul became the captain of the British merchant ship, *John*. During a **mutiny** on his ship, he killed a sailor. To avoid a trial, he fled to the **colonies** and changed his name to John Paul Jones.

Sailor for the Continental Army

At the start of the Revolutionary War, Jones traveled to Philadelphia to join the **Patriot** cause. On December 7, 1775, he was made a lieutenant in the Continental Navy. His first assignment was aboard the *Alfred*, under **Commodore** Esek Hopkins.

Town Crier News

- John Paul Jones's grave is at the U.S. Naval Academy Chapel in Annapolis, Maryland.

- He was originally buried in a small cemetery in Paris, France. When the U.S. government tried to find his gravesite, no one knew the exact location. In 1905, after six years of looking, his gravesite was found. The French gave the U.S. government permission to move Jones's body to Annapolis.

Captain Jones became a national hero.

Captain Jones commanded the Ranger *during the capture of the British warship* Drake *on April 24, 1778.*

Later, as captain of the Continental ship *Providence*, Jones successfully captured British merchant vessels. In 1777, he was appointed captain of the *Ranger*. He again helped the war effort by raiding British ports and merchant ships.

In 1779, Jones was promoted to commodore and given command of a new ship, the *Bon Homme Richard*. On September 23, 1779, the *Bon Homme Richard* went up against the British warship HMS *Serapis*. During this battle, Jones's ship sank, but the British warship surrendered.

Town Crier News

In 1778, the HMS *Drake* became the first British warship to surrender to the Continental Navy.

After the War

After the Revolutionary War, John Paul Jones served in the Russian Navy for a short time. In 1790, he went to live in Paris. He died two years later.

Admiral Lord Richard Howe (1726–1799)

Richard Howe was the commander of the British Naval forces for the British during the Revolutionary War. That meant he was the highest-ranking naval officer.

Before the Revolutionary War

Richard Howe was born in London, England, in 1726. He joined the British Navy at the young age of fourteen and was made a captain at age twenty.

During the Revolutionary War

In 1776, Howe replaced **Admiral** Samuel Graves as commander of the British Naval forces in North America. His brother, Sir William Howe, was in charge of the British Army in the North American **colonies.** The British Ministry hoped that the brothers could convince the colonists to agree to a settlement that would end the fighting. They were not able to do so.

Richard Howe was a skilled and daring commander. He defeated the French fleet of Comte d'Estaing at Newport, Rhode Island in 1778. This gave the British control of the Atlantic Ocean at the time.

Town Crier News

After the Revolutionary War, Richard Howe continued to serve in the British Navy. In 1788, he received the distinguished title of Baron.

Throughout his career in the British Navy, Admiral Howe won many sea battles against the French Navy. King George III of England rewarded Howe by making him a knight. This honor was usually given only to royalty.

Importance of Naval Battles

During the Revolutionary War, most of the American population lived within 100 miles (161 kilometers) of the ocean. Whoever controlled the ocean controlled the colonies. Both armies depended on their navies to provide supplies and transportation.

The few ships of the newly formed Continental Navy were no match for the established large fleet of the British Navy. The colonials' only hope for winning the war was to form an **alliance** with the powerful French. France agreed to send troops and ships to help the colonists defeat the British.

September 3, 1783

The Treaty of Paris, signed on September 3, 1783, brought independence for the United States from Great Britain. It also forced the development of a national army and navy. The challenge ahead would be for the United States to grow as an independent nation.

*An initial peace agreement between the Americans and the British was reached late in 1782. The official peace treaty was signed on September 3, 1783. As each man signed, he pressed his personal **seal** into the red wax. This showed that it was his genuine signature.*

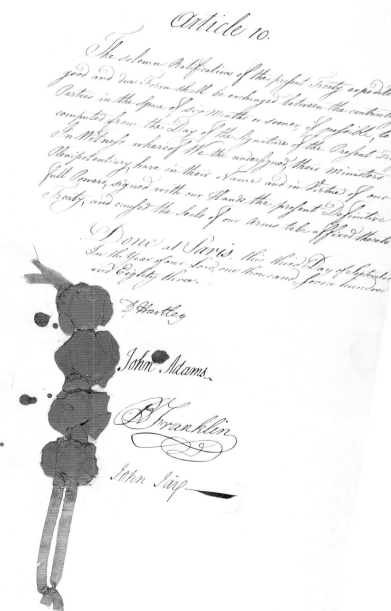

Town Crier News

On the same day that the United States won its independence, Great Britain also signed separate treaties with France and Spain in the city of Versailles, France.

Glossary

admiral   commander in chief of a navy

alliance   political agreement between two or more groups

artillery   cannons

blockade   troops or warships that block enemy troops or supplies from entering or leaving an area

bow   front of a ship

broadside   single side of a ship on which all cannons are located

colony   territory settled by people from other countries who still had loyalty to those other countries. The word *colonist* is used to describe a person who lives in a colony. The word *colonial* is used to describe things related to a colony.

commission   to officially approve the buying or building of ships for the U.S. Navy

commodore   high-ranking Continental Navy officer

Continental Congress   group of representatives from the colonies who carried out the duties of the government

convert   change from one thing to another

convoy   group of ships traveling together

frigate   type of sailing warship that was designed to go fast

isolated   away from any populated area

maneuverable   able to change direction easily

mast   tall pole on a sailing ship that holds the sails

mercenary   man fighting in a battle in order to earn money

merchant ship   ship that carries goods

mortar   cannon designed to shoot shells. They were used mainly to attack forts rather than ground troops.

mutiny   to turn against the person in charge

Patriot   person during colonial times who believed that the colonies should break away from the rule of Great Britain and form their own government

recruit   person who has agreed to sign up for something, usually military service

regular   full-time soldier

seal   symbol or signature pressed into wax to serve as proof that a signature was real

seam   small opening that may form when boards are joined side by side

siege   to surround an opposing army and capture it by bombing and blockading it

smuggle   to carry goods secretly

squadron   naval unit of two or more groups of ships

stern   back of a ship

Historical Fiction to Read

Denenberg, Barry. *The Journal of William Thomas Emerson: A Revolutionary War Patriot, Boston, Massachusetts, 1774.* New York: Scholastic, 1998.
A twelve-year-old orphan boy keeps a diary of his experiences before and during the Revolutionary War.

Schurfranz, Vivian. *A Message for General Washington.* New York: Silver Moon Press, 1998.
A twelve-year-old girl travels from her home in Yorktown, Virginia, to bring an important message to General George Washington.

Historical Places to Visit

Boston National Historical Park
Charlestown Navy Yard
Boston, Massachusetts 02129-4543
Visitor Information: (617) 242-5642
Take the Freedom Trail walking tour of the park to see sixteen Revolutionary War sites and structures. Visit downtown Boston to see the Old State House and the Paul Revere House. Visit Charlestown to see the Bunker Hill Monument.

Colonial National Historical Park
P.O. Box 210
Yorktown, Virginia 23690
Visitor Information: (757) 898-2410
Visit Yorktown, the site of the last major battle of the Revolutionary War in 1781.

Independence National Historical Park
313 Walnut Street
Philadelphia, Pennsylvania 19106
Visitor Information: (215) 597-8974
Visit the place where the Declaration of Independence and the U.S. Constitution were written. Tour downtown Philadelphia to see the Liberty Bell, Independence Hall, and other historical landmarks of the Revolutionary War.

Index